D1298836

THINGS THAT GO BUMP IN THE NIGHT!

WRITER: Todd Dezago
ARTISTS: Marcelo DiChiara
COLORS: Sotocolor
LETTERS: Dave Sharpe

SUPER HERO SQUAD STRIPS
WRITER: Paul Tobin
ARTISTS: Marcelo DiChiara, Todd Nauck & Dario Brizuela
COLORS: Chris Sotomayor
LETTERS: Blambot's Nate Piekos

ASSISTANT EDITOR: Michael Horwitz
EDITOR: Nathan Cosby

Spotlight

Visit us at www.abdopublishing.com

Reinforced library bound edition published in 2011 by Spotlight, a division of the ABDO Group, 8000 West 78th Street, Edina, Minnesota 55439. Spotlight produces high-quality reinforced library bound editions for schools and libraries. Published by agreement with Marvel Characters, Inc.

Printed in the United States of America, North Mankato, Minnesota.
102010
012011
This book contains at least 10% recycled materials.

Library of Congress Cataloging-in-Publication Data

Dezago, Todd.
Things that go bump in the night! / Todd Dezago, writer ; Marcelo DiChiara, artist ; Sotocolor, colors ; Dave Sharpe, letters. -- Reinforced library bound ed.
p. cm. -- (Super hero squad)
"Marvel."
ISBN 978-1-59961-862-3
1. Graphic novels. [1. Graphic novels. 2. Superheroes--Fiction.] I. Dichiara, Marcelo, ill. II. Title.
PZ7.7.D508Th 2011
741.5'973--dc22

2010027326

All Spotlight books have reinforced library bindings and are manufactured in the United States of America.

THE HULK IN:
HINGS THAT GO BUMP N THE NIGHT!
WORDS--TODD DEZAGO
PICTURES--MARCELO DICHIARA
COLORS--SOTOCOLOR
LETTERS--DAVE SHARPE
ASST EDITOR--MIKE HORWITZ
EDITOR--NATHAN COSBY
EDITOR-IN-CHIEF--JOE QUESADA
PUBLISHER--DAN BUCKLEY
EXECUTIVE PRODUCER--ALAN FINE
NUM-NUM-NUM-NUM-!
HULK LOVE ICE CREAM!
HULK LOVE BIRTHDAY CAKE!
HULK HAPPY!
NUM-NUM-NUM-NUM--
--HUH?
HELLO, HULK. IT'S ME--THE DENTIST! IT'S TIME FOR YOUR CLEANING!
HAVE YOU BEEN A GOOD BOY? YOU HAVEN'T BEEN EATING TOO MANY SWEETS, HAVE YOU? I HOPE WE DON'T FIND ANY CAVITIES!!
OPEN WIDE AND SAY--

AAAAHHHH!
NO, SCARY DENTIST--NO! HULK DON'T WANT TO! LEAVE HULK A--
--LONE?
HULK?! WHAT IS IT, SOLDIER? THAT SCREAM--I THOUGHT WE WERE UNDER ATTACK FROM DOOM'S LETHAL LEGION...
...OR THE BEDFORD FALLS SENIOR CITIZEN'S NEEDLEPOINT COMMITTEE--THEY'RE CRAFTY LITTLE BUGGERS...
HULK... HAD B-BAD DREAM.
SCARY DENTIST COME TO HURT HULK'S TEETH.
IS THAT ALL? NOTHING TO WORRY ABOUT, MY JOLLY GREEN COMRADE! NIGHTMARES ARE JUST OUR IMAGINATIONS PLAYING TRICKS ON US!
WE ALL KNOW THERE'S NO SUCH THINGS AS BOOGEYMEN OR DENTISTS.
CREEEAK!
AHHH! WHAT THAT?!
HA HA! JUST SOME CREAKS AND GROANS, HULK. THE HELICARRIER IS A GOOD OLD SHIP AND SHE MAKES A LOT OF STRANGE NOISES THAT WE DON'T HEAR DURING THE DAY.
REMEMBER, THERE'S AN EXPLANATION FOR EVERYTHING--
--DON'T LET YOURSELF BE SCARED BY THINGS THAT GO BUMP IN THE NIGHT.

THING GOING BUMP IN NIGHT...?
BUMP
THUMP
SQUEEEEEK

SHHRRIP
HULK DON'T LIKE THING GOING BUMP IN NIGHT!

TO TOPSIDE
LANDING DECK

THUDD!
...THING GO BUMP IN NIGHT...

HUH?... WHA...? SUE... DIDYOUHEAR SOMETHING...?

SCANNING FOR I.D.: HULK, THE INCREDIBLE.
I.D. CONFIRMED: GREETINGS, HULK. WELCOME TO THE BAXTER BUILDING.

...THING GO BUMP IN NIGHT...

PRIVATE
UARTERS

Benjamin J. Grimm

RACE
HUH...? WHA...? WUZZAT...? 'ZAT YOU, HULK?

POW!
...THAT'S A LOVELY DRESS YOU'RE WEARING, AUNT PETUNIA...
WHA--? WHA HAPPENED...?
THING STOP GOING BUMP IN NIGHT--MAKING HULK MAD--GIVING HULK BAD DREAMS.
THE EN

REPTIL IN--
April's Fool!
TODD DEZAGO WRITER
MARCELO DICHIARA ARTIST
SOTOCOLOR COLORS
DAVE SHARPE LETTERS
MIKE HORWITZ ASST EDITOR
NATHAN COSBY EDITOR
JOE QUESADA EDITOR IN CHIEF
DAN BUCKLEY PUBLISHER
ALAN FINE EXECUTIVE PRODUCER
APRIL
1
OH, MAN! THIS IS GONNA BE AWESOME!
APRIL FOOLS DAY IS THE ONE DAY YOU CAN PULL A PRANK ON SOMEONE AND NOT GET BUSTED FOR IT!
I'VE BEEN PLANNING FOR WEEKS AND I'VE GOT ALL THE STUFF I'LL NEED...
Haulin' Oats Oatmeal
GreasyLube
PETROLEUM JELLY

FIRST, WE PUT A LITTLE GREASYLUBE ON THE HANDLE OF THOR'S HAMMER SO, WHEN HE GOES TO GRAB FOR IT--SLIP!-- HE CAN'T EVEN PICK IT UP!
ZZZZZZ
SOME OF THE SAME STUFF ON THE SURFER'S BOARD AND HE'S GONNA SLIDE AROUND LIKE HE'S ON SUPER HERO CITY'S FUNNIEST HOME VIDEOS--!

WHILE IRON MAN'S IN THE SHOWER, WE SERVE HIM BREAKFAST--IN HIS ARMOR! WHEN HE PUTS ON HIS BOOTS AND HELMET--GWISH!
HA HA! MAN, I WISH I COULD SEE HIS FACE WHEN HE EATS THAT!
AND I NEVER THOUGHT I'D BE THANKFUL FOR THAT SEWING CLASS IN INDUSTRIAL ARTS, BUT NOTHING IS GONNA BE FUNNIER THAN WOLVIE IN HIS UNIFORM THIS MORNING...
...NOW THAT I'VE MADE A FEW... ALTERATIONS! NYUCK NYUCK!
THE FALCON ISN'T HERE, SO I DIDN'T HAFTA PLAN ANYTHING FOR HIM...
AND... SSSSHHHH!--I LEARNED A LONG TIME AGO THAT IT'S NOT REALLY HEALTHY TO PULL A PRANK ON THE HULK...!
HEE HEE HEE
SPLOOOSH
GRRRR--
ULP! WAIT, I--I'M...I'M STUCK!
SOMEBODY...?
ANYBODY...?
JEEZ--WHAT'S WITH ALL THESE FEATHERS...?
ONE OF THE SERVICE-DROIDS MUST'VE BEEN DUSTING THE HALLWAYS WITH A MOLTING FEATHER DUSTER...!

AHHH...NOW THAT EVERYTHING'S IN PLACE, ALL I HAVE TO DO IS SIT BACK AND WATCH THE HILARITY BEGI--
WHOOMP! WHOOMP! WHOOMP! WHOOMP
INTRUDER ALERT! INTRUDER ALERT!
INTRUDER ALERT! INTRUDER ALERT!
INTRUDER ALERT! INTRUDER ALERT!
WHA--?! WAIT--WHAT?! WHAT'S GOING ON?! WHAT'S HAPPENING?!
INTRUDER ALERT! INTRUDER ALERT!
INTRUDER ALERT! INTRUDER ALERT!
INTRUDER IDENTIFIED AS CHTYLOK--THE CHICKEN-COW!! DANGER! DANGER! SUPER HERO SQUAD IN DANGER! HERO UP! HERO UP!
SWEET STEGOSAURUS! WHAT DO I DO?! WHAT DO I DO?!
THE CHTYLOK?! I'VE--I'VE NEVER EVEN HEARD OF HIM!
CHTYLOK-- CHE-K'N KAU-- CHICKEN-COW SUBTERRANEAN MONSTER OF IMMENSE POWER! CALLING ALL SQUADDIES!
CALLING ALL SQUADDIES!
HECK, BETTER CALL THE FANTASTIC FOUR, TOO! AND THE X-MEN! AND GORILLA MAN! AND YER AUNT PETUNIA!
COULD SOMEBODY UNPLUG ME...?
BUT THE COMPUTER SAYS THAT HE'S ONE OF THE BIGGEST AND BADDEST MONSTERS WE'VE EVER FACED! AND NOW HE'S HERE ON THE SHIP! AND...
ZOUNDS! THAT BLARING KLAXON HAST PUT AN END TO MY BEAUTY SLEEP! OF WHAT INTRUDER DOST IT SCREAM...?
...AND, OH, NO! WHAT HAVE I DONE?!
ODIN'S IPOD! THE CHICKEN-COW?! TO ME, MIGHTLY MJOLNIR! TO BATTLE THIS EVIL BEAST WE WILL NEED ALL OF OUR--
WHATETH THE--?! MINE HAMMER FLIES FROM MY GRASP AS IF T'WERE COATED WITH DRAGON-GREASE! SURELY THERE IS SABOTAGE AFOOT!
ZWIIIP!

WHOA! MY FRIENDS, IS THIS TRUE? HAS THE VILE CHICKEN-COW GAINED ACCESS TO OUR FLOATING FORTRESS?
I SHALL SUMMON MY BOARD AND INVESTIGATE HOW THE BEAST MAY HAVE--
WHOA! WHOA! WHOA-WHOA-WHOA-WHOA-WHOA!
OOF!
BONK!
SLIP! SLIP! SLIPPY-SLIP!
I'M TELLIN' YA, THIS HAD BETTER BE THE WORK OF SOME CRAZY, DERANGED, FASHION-IMPAIRED SUPER VILLAIN, 'CAUSE IF THAT KID HAD SOMETHIN' TO DO WITH THIS, I'M GONNA--
LOOK OUT! GANGWAY! RUNAWAY ARMOR!
CAN'T SEE! CAN'T SEE! LOOK OUT!
HUH? WHAT--?
PLOP!
BLOP!
BLORP!
OH, NO!
LOOK OUT! CAN'T SEE!
WHAMM!
UNGH!
KRAAWWW! KRAWWW!

KRAWWWWW! KRAWWWW!
NO! NO NO NO NO--I-I-I NEVER MEANT FOR THIS TO HAPPEN!...
WHAT HAVE I DONE?! WHAT HAVE I DONE?!
HA HA HA HA HA! LOBSTER FALL FOR BEST APRIL FOOL JOKE EVER!!
HA HA HA!!
WHAT...? WHAT?!
WE HEARD THAT YOU WERE PLANNIN' A LITTLE APRIL FOOL'S DAY SOMETHIN'-SOMETHIN' FOR US... SO WE THOUGHT WE'D PUT TOGETHER A LITTLE SOMETHIN' FOR YOU AND BEAT YA TO IT!
APRIL FOOLS, REPTIL!
AND HERE'S THE FUNNIEST PART, 'BERTO--APRIL FOOLS DAY IS ALSO APRIL FIRST--
--AND YOU KNOW MS. MARVEL LIKES TO MAKE HER INSPECTION OF THE HELICARRIER ON THE FIRST OF EVERY MONTH...SO YOU BETTER GET CLEANING!
AND SHE LIKES EVERYTHING TO SHINE.
THE END!

CAPTAIN AMERICA
SENTINEL OF LIBERTY,
AND THE HIGH-FLYING
FALCON
TOGETHER AGAIN-- FOR THE FIRST TIME!
FALCON DOESN'T LISTEN. HE'S WILD AND DOESN'T ALWAYS FOLLOW ORDERS.
WHY, IF WE HAD A SOLDIER LIKE THAT BACK IN THE BIG ONE*, WE'D PAINT HIM GREEN, PUT HIM IN A BOX, AND SHIP HIM BACK TO "STRAIGHTEN-UP-SOLDIERVILLE!"
UH... RIGHT.
*WORLD WAR II-- KNOW-IT-ALL NATE.
SURE, CAP IS AN AMERICAN ICON. HE BEAT THE NAZIS IN WORLD WAR II*! BUT, HE'S A LITTLE... LOOPY, KNOW WHAT I'M SAYIN'?
I MEAN, DOES HE EVEN KNOW WHAT YEAR IT IS?
UH... RIGHT...
*SEE? I TOLD YA-- NYA-NAH-NAH-NAH-NATE
DAYS LATER, HOWEVER, WHEN CAPTAIN AMERICA AND FALCON ARE THE ONLY TWO HEROES ON-DECK--
ATTENTION, SUPER HERO SQUAD! WE HAVE SOMETHING OF YOURS--SOMETHING VERY PRECIOUS! AND YOU'LL BRING THREE FRACTALS TO THE TOWN SQUARE IN 20 MINUTES...
...IF YOU EVER WANT TO SEE YOUR PET BIRD AGAIN!
WHIRLWIND!
CRIMSON DYNAMO!
REDWING!
STEADY, SOLDIER. DON'T GIVE IN TO THEIR TAUNTS. YOU AND I WILL GO TAKE CARE OF THIS TOGETHER. DON'T WORRY--WE'LL GET YOUR PIGEON BACK.

ORTLY AT TOWN SQUARE...
THERE THEY ARE, CAP! JUST LET ME GO, I'LL--
EASY, FALCON. I TOLD YOU, I HAVE A PLAN.
THE RED ONE IS A RUSSIAN IRON MAN WANNABE--AND THE GREEN ONE IS AN IRON MAN WANNABE THAT SPINS AROUND... LIKE MY UNCLE CURLY WHEN HE ATE SOME BAD CHEESE...
BUT IN THE END, THEY'RE JUST A COUPLE OF BULLIES. THEY'RE DESTINED FOR DEFEAT.
BIG
NOW YOU'RE HERE! HAND OVER THE FRACTALS!
IF YOU'VE HURT ONE FEATHER--
FALCON. REMEMBER WHAT I SAID...
HERE YOU ARE, GENTLEMEN.
WHA--?! BANANAS?! WHAT IS THIS?!
A GREAT SOURCE OF POTASSIUM AND AN EXCELLENT BOOST OF ENERGY TO START YOUR DAY.
CAPTAIN AMERICA DOESN'T NEGOTIATE WITH BULLIES--
NOW IF YOU'LL JUST HAND OVER REDWING AND COME WITH US, WE'LL--
THEY'RE GETTING AWAY!
YOU GET WHIRLPOOL! I'LL TAKE CARE OF CHRISTMAS DYNAMITE!

WHIRLWIND?! BUT THE DYNAMO HAS REDWING!
I SHOULD-- NO. I'M GONNA LISTEN TO CAP.
HA! GOT YOU! FOLLOWING ORDERS AND NOT PAYING ATTENTION, BIRD-BRAIN!
GAH! NO! DYNAMO CAUGHT ME!
FALCON-- DUCK!
UNGH!
KLANG!
DUCK?! WHAT DOES--
SCREEEEE!
REDWING!

CAP! WHIRLWIND! HE'S GETTING AWAY!
NOT TODAY.
KLICK!
SPANG!
KLANG!
WHOOOOSH!
OH, NO!
CAP, I...YOU... YOU...YOU WERE AMAZING! YOU SAVED REDWING! THAT WAS YOUR PLAN ALL ALONG, RIGHT? TO GET ME CLOSE ENOUGH TO CATCH REDWING?! THAT WAS AWESOME!
YOU DID A GOOD JOB YOURSELF, FALCON. YOU FOLLOWED ORDERS AND THE PLAN CAME TOGETHER PERFECTLY! MAYBE THERE'S HOPE FOR YOU YET.
NOW WHAT SAY WE GO GRAB A COUPLE SODA-POPS... AND MAYBE WE CAN FIND SOME CRACKERS FOR YOUR PARROT.
SCREEEE?
?
WRITER: TODD DEZAGO
ARTIST: MARCELO DICHIARA
COLORIST: SOTOCOLOR
LETTERER: DAVE SHARPE
PRODUCTION: JEFF POWELL
ASST. EDITOR: MICHAEL HORWITZ
EDITOR: NATHAN COSBY
EDITOR IN CHIEF: JOE QUESADA
PUBLISHER: DAN BUCKLEY
EXECUTIVE PRODUCER: ALAN FINE
THE END.

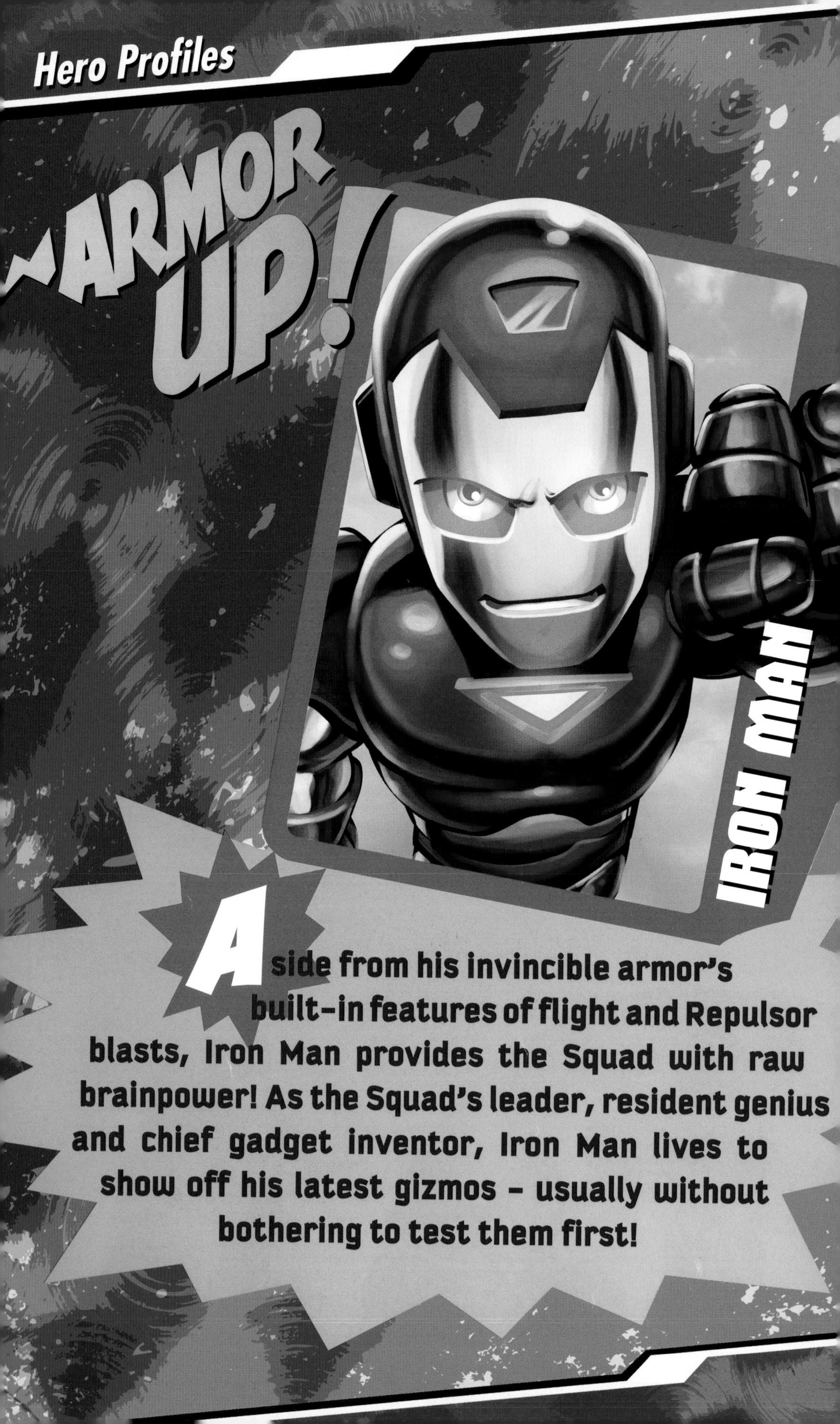

Aside from his invincible armor's built-in features of flight and Repulsor blasts, Iron Man provides the Squad with raw brainpower! As the Squad's leader, resident genius and chief gadget inventor, Iron Man lives to show off his latest gizmos - usually without bothering to test them first!

He's the best soldier since Captain America, and Falcon puts his tactical skills to good use as the Squad's aerial expert. His "Hard Light" wing harness enables him to soar the skies at unbelievable speeds, and his ability to communicate with birds makes him a natural for high-flying reconnaissance missions. Just don't tell anyone he's actually afraid of heights!

AWWW, DUDE! THAT'S CHEATING!

DOOM'S RECRUITMENT PROCESS: THE EARLY DAYS.
WILL WORK FOR FOOD
WILL SMASH GOOD GUYS FOR FOOD